FROGGY PLAYS IN THE BAND

ROGGY PLAYS
IN THE BAND

by JONATHAN LONDON
illustrated by FRANK REMKIEWICZ

PUFFIN BOOKS

For Emma, Hannah, Leah, Max, D.J., Stephanie, Maia, and Sean—
and for Becky Martin and the Willowside School Band.
    —J. L.

For Froggy's *other* band: Cecilia, Denise, Nina, Teresa, Creston, and Victoria.
    —F. R.

PUFFIN BOOKS
Published by Penguin Group
Penguin Young Readers Group,
345 Hudson Street, New York, New York 10014, U.S.A.
Penguin Books Ltd, 80 Strand, London WC2R ORL, England
Penguin Books Australia Ltd, 250 Camberwell Road, Camberwell, Victoria 3124, Australia
Penguin Books Canada Ltd, 10 Alcorn Avenue, Toronto, Ontario, Canada M4V 3B2
Penguin Books (N.Z.) Ltd, 182-190 Wairau Road, Auckland 10, New Zealand

First published in the United States of America by Viking, a division of Penguin Putnam Books for Young Readers, 2002
Published by Puffin Books, a division of Penguin Young Readers Group, 2004

30 29 28 27 26 25 24 23

THE LIBRARY OF CONGRESS HAS CATALOGED THE VIKING EDITION AS FOLLOWS:
London, Jonathan, 1947—
Froggy plays in the band / by Jonathan London ; illustrated by Frank Remkiewicz.
p. cm.
Summary: Froggy's marching band practices for their debut at the Apple Blossom Parade, hoping to win the big prize.
ISBN 0-670-03532-7 (hc)
[1. Marching Bands—Fiction. 2. Bands (Music)—Fiction. 3. Contests—Fiction. 4. Parades—Fiction.
5. Frogs—Fiction. 6. Animals—Fiction.] I. Remkiewicz, Frank, ill. II. Title.
PZ7.L8432 Frn 2002 [E]—dc21 2001005037

Puffin Books ISBN 978-0-14-240051-7

Manufactured in China
Set in Kabel

At school one day,
Froggy read a sign.
It said . . .

"Great!" said Froggy.
"A band contest!"

He flopped over to see Miss Martin,
the music teacher—*flop flop flop.*
"What's the big prize?" asked Froggy.
"It's a surprise!" she said.
"If you and your friends start a marching band,
and compete against other schools in the
Apple Blossom Parade—you can win the prize!"

"What will I play?" wondered Froggy.
Then he remembered his dad's old sax.

And after school,
he flopped up to the attic—*flop flop flop*—
and started blowing his dad's horn—
honk! bleep! screeeeeech!

FRROOGGYY!

called his dad.
"Wha–a–a t?"
"Quiet please! I'm on the phone!"

"I'm on the phone, too," cried Froggy.
"The *SAX*ophone!"—*honk!*

Next day, Froggy got his band together
and they practiced in his yard.
Max on drums—*ka-BOOM!*
Leah on triangle—*ting-a-ling!*
Emma on recorder—*tweedle-dee!*
And Hannah, her twin, on cymbals—*CLASH!*

"I want to join, too!" said Frogilina.
"What do *you* play?" asked Froggy.
"Nothing," she said. "But I can do *this*."
And she twirled a baton,
tossed it high into the air . . .

and caught it behind her back!—"Ta-*da!*"

Every day after school, Froggy's Ragtag Band
marched around and around the playground—
Honk! ka-BOOM! ting-a-ling! tweedle-dee! CLASH!

And every day, Miss Martin told them the rules for marching:
"Don't look left.
Don't look right.
And DON'T STOP FOR ANYTHING!"

"What if you have to go to the bathroom?"
asked Froggy.
"DON'T STOP FOR *ANYTHING*!"
commanded Miss Martin.
"Or everybody behind you
will crash into you!"

Three weeks left.

Two weeks.

One.

Froggy practiced marching everywhere—
even in his sleep.

At last, the big day came.
The apple trees had burst into bloom,
and the parade was ready to begin.
Everybody was nervous—
especially Froggy.

Miss Martin said, "Now remember:
    Don't look left.
    Don't look right.
        And DON'T STOP FOR ANYTHING!
And the parade began.

Being the youngest,
 Froggy's band marched in front,
  led by the majorette—
   the one and only Frogilina.

FRROOGGYY!

called his father—
he was jumping up and down
on the sidelines.
But Froggy didn't look.

FRROOGGYY!

called his mother—
she was aiming a camera.

But Froggy didn't look.
Cameras flashed. Clowns threw candy.
And still Froggy marched, looking straight ahead.
Here came the judges' stand.
This was the big moment!

Frogilina twirled her baton.
She tossed it high into the air . . .
and Froggy thought:
    Don't look left.
    Don't look right.
    And—

BONK! Her baton hit him on the head and knocked him down.
"Oops!" cried Froggy, looking more red in the face than green.
Oof! Clang! Crash!—
and the rest of the parade piled on.

FRROOGGYY!

called Miss Martin.
"Wha-a-a-t?" came a muffled cry.
"Are you all right?"

Froggy crawled out
from the bottom of the heap,
and said, "DON'T STOP FOR ANYTHING!"
and started to wail a wild swamp tune
on his saxophone.

The rest of his band joined in,
and everybody danced in the street!
And when the judges' vote came in . . .
Froggy's Ragtag Band had won a *special* award:
  COOLEST MARCHING BAND
  AT THE APPLE BLOSSOM PARADE.

"What's the big prize?" asked Froggy.
"This is!" said Frogilina.
And she gave him a big juicy kiss
smack on his cheek—*EEEEEEEEEK!*

Then the judges gave Froggy and his band
the *real* prize—a big golden trophy
in the shape of a saxophone.

"*Yes!*" cried Froggy.
And Froggy's Ragtag Band
played one last time—
Honk! ka-BOOM! ting-a-ling! tweedle-dee! CLASH!